Mantle of Gods

Book 2

Dragon Academy

By

Christopher M Delano

Dragon List.

1. Martin- Prismatic Dragon- Swirl

2. Calypso- Yellow Dragon- Topaz

3. Cady- Prismatic Dragon- Rainbow

4. Caleb- Blue Dragon- Sapphire

5. Zach- Red Dragon- Sparks

6. Sky- Prismatic Dragon- Prism

7. Dragon Knight- Red Dragon- Blaze

8. Sam-   Blue   and   Pink   Speckles
   Dragon- Sparkle

9. Taylor- White Dragon- Frost

10. Mike- Black Dragon- Shadow

11. Hiro- Crystal Dragon- Glimmer

12. Rufus- Brown Dragon- Dusty

13. Ken- Silver Dragon- Quick

14. Sophie- Silver Dragon- Silva

15. Gustof- Brass Dragon- Half-Pint

16. Mary- Gold Dragon- Heart- Dragon Queen

17. Lance- Bronze Dragon- Shine

18. Melanie- Green Dragon- Forest

19. Mina- White Dragon- Snowflake

20. -Red Dragon- Flicker

21. - White Dragon- Periwinkle

22. Daisy- Yellow Dragon- Sunflower

23. Bruce- Blue Dragon- Bolt

Prologue

Martin, Calypso, Cady, Caleb, Zach, and Sky step out of the portal. The most remote place in the USA. Martin plans the last Grove seed and watches the mighty oak grow. Buildings start to appear. Martin starts his trip around the Grove to enchant rooms and chests to hold more stuff and tolerate breaking of things. He charms the pantry with a Cornucopia spell so it always produces natural food for dragons and humans alike. He snaps the dragon token. But nothing happens. Everyone waits here. I will be back soon.

Chapter 1

He teleports to New York Harbor and charters
a boat. He cast the spell for Avalon. Mist takes
him directly to the cave where the Dragon
Knight lives and he begins to walk across the
water.

Greeting, Dragon Knight says Martin.

Please just Erik.

What is wrong?

Blaze won't get up. I fear he has been sleeping
too long.
Let's have a look. Fey magic is interesting but
strange. Swirl come out. I am going to need
you. Swirl hops out.

He is sick, he talks to the world and I can smell

it.

What is it?

Dragon Rot. Only a Moon Pod can save him now.

Where do I find that?

Ask the Gods they should know.

Mercury or Isis is who I would check with, the Mantle says.

How long does he have?

In Avalon 2 maybe 3 days.

I will be back. He heads for the boat and then back to the harbor.

He calls Mercury.

Yes, what can I do for you?

I need a Moon Pod.

It is ancient and has no curative properties.

I was told it will cure Dragon Rot.

That it will but Isis is the keeper of that stuff not me.

I guess I will just have to visit Egypt and see. Have that boy ready for me. The Academy opens in 2 days as long as the teacher has a healthy dragon.

Just let me know where.

The hospital.

I get him there to see if he can be chosen. It is not magic school for him.

Good I let you be surprised. Ok.

In Egypt: Greeting leader what can I do for you, Isis says?

I need a Moon Pod.

They are rare.

There are only 3 in this dimension.

What is your scheme and are you working?

Just trying to save a dragon.

There one that the Buddha temple in Budapest seeing as you beat up the owner I doubt he will give it to you. The other 2 are hidden and only can be found by Moon Beam holders. There has not been one of those in a while.

I guess I am going to Buddapest.

So your back, stealing my power was not good enough The One God Says.

I want the Moon Pod.

No I won't let you have it.

I need it to save a dragon.

What do you want?

I want power.

I will restore the Buddha to you. Bring me the Moon Pod and I will grant you the tranquility of the Buddha and you live out the rest of your days in peace here.

It is not power. It is the power of peace.

I am not even sure it is going to work. But I will try to save a dragon.

Fine. He runs to the and returns with a small flower. Be Careful, it 's delicate.

Remember I'll give you the Lotus Blossom. You have to eat it. You either become the Buddha or be burnt.

As soon as the Lotus touches his lips, fire engulfs him. I guess you were not peaceful enough. As he scoops up the Lotus Blossom and phases back to the boat.

He asked Mercury and Swirl what to do and soon a potion was brewed. He takes the boat back to Avalon. Appearing at the cave. I got it. We just have to rub it into the scales.

That's it.

Soon they rub it into the scales as they brighten. Soon a roar sounds.

Let us meet the youngsters.

I still have to pick them. There are 2 kids, 2 teenagers, and a titan so far.

Interesting choice, the dragons all choose for themselves.

I know already about the choosing of a dragon. I was 7 and when I found his egg in the family barn. Every color has an emotional choice. Red for instance looks for angry or passionate people. Prismatic looks for organized chaos. So on. When class starts I will explain more. I assume you have a boat.

That I do.

Come on big fella. Blaze disappears.

They take the boat back to New York. He poofs them to the Grove.

Chapter 2

Hello this is Erik. He is the last living Dragon Knight. He is going to share some knowledge tonight. Tomorrow I go recruiting for the first hundred. I am from every major country. The news has already spread the meeting location. I just have to bounce around to get them. There are a lot of pocket dimensions and extra dimensional space. All the rooms are their own dimension but they are limited in space. All the storage is extra-dimensional also.

Interesting.

Why?

There is not enough space for everyone and their dragons in this dimension. Let me show you to your room.

I hope it has a cave.

It has a cave in it. Just like all the pocket dimensions.

Good cause all I had was a cave for a thousand years. Plus dragons prefer them.

So this is my new home.

The door will only open for me and you. So you do not have to worry about the company.

Thank you.

I am off to my wife.

The building has all you two can eat. I am working on having game brought in so the dragons can hunt.

That a smart decision.

Just keep an eye on the random game just showing up. See you in the morning.

He walks to his wife playing fetch with Topaz.

He seems a little off.

You would too if all you had for company was a

sleeping dragon.

I guess I had heros and arts and crafts.

Plus you have my personal knowledge of the

world.

He does not.

All he knows is what he saw in a fey mirror.

So he is the evil queen.

This is not Snow White.

I got to get the boy in the hospital in the morning. Then start testing people.

Ok then let's go to bed. Where are you going first?

Chicago I think. Depends on how long the boy at the hospital takes. Good night.

Good Morning beautiful.

I'll be recieve anyone you send.

Good.

Try to keep the gender balanced.

I do not pick, you know that.

He receives a text.

I want a dragon but can't make the meeting point.

Where are you?

Hospital in Tennessee.

I will try to come to you if there is time. What is your name?

Taylor. The Mantle lights at her name

You are meant for something great.

Thank you.

I look forward to seeing you.

Who was that?

Just someone who wants to come but can't make the meeting.

You're going to go to her.

Of course. Transportation or economic status should stop the selection process.

Good I am glad.

We need to get up and get dressed. He showers and comes out in a long flowing robe. Too much he asks.

Not for this.

Good.

Let's meet the other for breakfast. They all sit and eat. I remind the kids to behave before leaving.

He poofs to Baton Rouge to meet Mercury.
How is he doing?
Better without the cancer. But there something I should tell you, there something even I can't fix.

Anything I can do?

Listen and figure it out.

This is the room.

Good morning young man. As femine voice replies.

So the doctor didn't tell you.

Why would I it your secret?

Since you save me. I am both genders. I have both parts and depending on hormone levels things about me change. My name is Sam not Samantha or Samuel just Sam.

How old are you?

16 and pathetic.

Why say that?

I live in a hospital and should be dead but between you and the doctor I get to live.

Have you seen the announcement on TV?

Yea but I am not that lucky.

Let's start simple, how would your hair like your back?

Straight, Black, and Shoulder length.

He rubs her scalp and the hair starts to grow.

Awesome. I have not had hair in years.

Here a brush. Wanna try your luck in my sack of eggs.

Sure. In a moment she pulls out a speckled egg and it starts to crack.

This is Sparkle. Your very own dragon. Let's turn the hospital gown into traveling clothes. Jeans and a speckled shirt appear. Ready to go.

I guess where to?

He texted Taylor.

What Room?

1183.

He gets directions from the desk. Knock.

So you did come. You brought your daughter?

No another trainee. I picked her up from another hospital.

Hey Sam says.

I am not going to lie. Let's start with what is wrong.

Lung infection.

Phoenix I summon you. Heal this girl.

Fire washes over her.

I can breathe.

Your disease is free, up for trying your luck and picking a dragon.

She reaches in and pulls out a white egg. It looks like a chicken egg.

Just give it a rub.

She does and white snout pops out.

He is Frost.

Soon you will both be able to talk to one another.

How old are you?

24.

Good you do not need permission to leave.

Do you have clothes?

If you turn around.

Ok ready.

She dressed in a white sundress.

Where are we going?

Chicago to start the selection process.

Chapter 3

He portals and appears in the middle of Wrigley's Field. Everyone can hear me. The selection process is to walk up, reach your hand in the bag, and either come out with a dragon and go to school, or leave here empty handed. Any questions before we begin. First up Lee and no draw happens. The first 20 don't pick an egg. Number 22 Mike picks a black egg and black snout pokes out. He is Shadow just stepping through that door. You'll be at your new home. Off he goes. In total there 4 yellow, 2 blue, and 3 prismatics from the Chicago selection.

Next he portals to Japan. A young man draws a Crystal Dragon. Congratulations. You are? Hiro Masasume.
Just step through. The dragon selection goes through 75 people come out with 4 blues, 3 red and 2 white.

He portals to Australia next. Around the 15 selection a brown egg is chosen. Out pops Dusty.

I am Rufus.

Just step through and you will be at your new home. This selection comes up with 9 brown dragons.

He portals to China and it takes 3 draws to find the first dragon. A Silver Dragon is drawn from the sack. Well introduce yourself.

I am Ken.

This is Quick. The selections goes 4 silver, 2 lung, 1 brown, 1 red, and 1 blue.

He shots into Russia and the second draw pulls a Silver Dragon. This is Silva and I am Martin. Who are you?

I am Sophie.

Tell me your parents are here.

Right in front.

So she has permission to go.

Here the documents you requested online.

Thank you just step through the portal. This selection yields 4 silver and 5 white. Girls there 2 stop in Europe. You can step through if you are   tired.

We are fine, they say.

We have Germany and Ireland, then there are 2 stops after that. Then we head to your new home.

They portal to Germany and a man steps up.

I am Gustof and I make beer.

Nice to meet you I am Martin. Just reach in and see what happens. He pulls out a dull metallic egg. It hatches to reveal a brass dragon. His name is Half-Pint. I am not sure if you will ever ride him but your welcome at school.

Thank you as he walks through the portal. Selection in Germany yields 4 copper, 4 brass, and 1 red.

Martin thinks to himself that all that he needs is a still.

He portals to Ireland and runs across an irish lass.

I want to meet you but the men would not let me in the show. Saying I am too young to ride a dragon.

How old are you?

Mary 17

Old enough for the purposes. Here pick one.

She pulls out a Golden egg.

Your special. I only have 4 of those eggs left. It hatches. Hello Heart. She will take good care of you. Just step through and she is gone.

He addresses the crowd. These events are not denied to anyone. I learned that you denied access to a young lady on my here. If you are trying to prevent the young or the females from taking part in the event. Dont. I will know. I will be back after my trip to Africa. Now make this right and I will be back.

He and the 2 girls poof to Africa where a crowd awaits. Their selection is about to start. This selection is time consuming. There are 50 people and still no dragons have appeared. A black male comes up. Who are you?

Lance Manby and I have come for a dragon. I have been here since I got the message.

Reach in and try. He pulls out a Bronze Dragon Egg. Shine pokes his head out as he shows the crowd. Just step through the portal. This selection seems to take forever as thousands try to get a dragon as the 9 are selected. 3 bronze, 3 brass, and 3 brown are hatched.

Martin and the girls poof back to Ireland to see a crowd mixed with kids and women. This selection goes quick. 4 men, 3 women, and 2 teenagers selecting 4 bronze, 2 prismatic, 2 green, and a blue. Let's grab some dinner girls. They stop at a restaurant and get fish and chips. Martin pays in gold and leaves.

They portal into a clearing in the middle of the rainforest.

Sorry sir but no adults believe the message.

And how old are you?

I am Melanie and I am 17.

I helped get the kids and other teens here.

I guess you get to pick first. She selects a green egg that hatches into a Green Dragon named Forest. 9 other teens get Green Dragons. Martin tells the kids to just let him touch them and they will wake up in their bed.

Chapter 4

As the portal opens to mountains they all step out. How is everything here Calypso?

Good except the girl with the Gold Dragon is in a foul mood that she is not living in luxury.

Help these ones out and I will see what I can do with her. Mary is it. I am told your not happy with your living arrangement

I miss my soft bed and my clothes.

Have you talked to Heart yet.

No why?

She has the power to give all that and more? You just have to tap in the power of Heart and you can make almost anything. Show me your room and we will see what Heart can do. They appear in the third biggest room in the female dorm. Focus on Heart and draw her power into you. Once you have it, just focus on what you want to change. Soon the room changes to a golden mess. Too much power and not enough focus. Before you ask, gold is a good color but sucks to sleep on. Keep trying if you do not get it by lights out call me.

Yes Sir.

Remember detail counts. As he walks out of the dorms.

We have an issue Calypso states! What do I do with just Sam?

Put her in the teacher's room for now. Most are open.

Ok. That sounds close to plan.

It is the best I can do without making her a private building for her. You should talk to her. Explain the options and let her decide.

I will. He finds Sam skipping rocks and asks wanna talk about it.

I have my own room but I am uncomfortable sharing a shower or even a bathroom in front of people.

There are 2 options. Option 1 is I put in the teacher's rooms which all have their own private bathroom. Option 2 is I build your private house and you're all by yourself.

Teacher's room is fine. At least I might fit in there.

Ok. Do you have anything to move?

No.

Then I will show you one.

They walk to the main building. Room 3 is yours. What do you think? Once you learn to control Sparkle's power. I'll show you how to make things, like a new wardrobe.

That's a lot of dresses. Is it really as easy as you make it seem.

Think of something simple. The more detail you can think of the better it will turn out but it is harder to do. Then just tap in to the connection with Sparkle.

A leather collar appears in her hand. Can you help?

It is a good piece.

It reminds me of a piece I wore for halloween before my Dad died.

Keep it up and soon you will build your own house somewhere.

Thank you.

He goes to find Calypso.

Everything is sorted and settled. Zach seemed to be a good leader.

Good I am glad. So school started tomorrow

Yes, so the plan is to break up into groups and learn the basis as they learn. Then send them to Erik for advanced training. By then I am hoping the older kids and adults can help the younger ones.

I can't do sounds as the bell rings.

I will go help her and I will be back. Mary show me what you are doing.

The whole room changes.

You're doing too much. Try to focus on one item at time. Start with something small like the sheets.

She concentrates and Egyptain cotton sheets appear.

Now the frame.

The bed changes into a 4 poster canopy bed.

Good now just focus on one item at a time and work on completing the room. Here a snack and don't forget to sleep.

Thank you.

Your Welcome as he poofs to his room.

What happened?

Just someone trying to do too much too quickly.

Oh!

How is the setup for magic item making going?

Someone made it more efficient.

That's good.

Let's get some sleep.

Chapter 5

The next morning: As most of you can tell your dragons are bigger and hungrier. You need to eat and feed them even more than you do now. We will go over hygiene after breakfast. That massive door leads to a cleaning station.

They walk through to a massive lake. First we will do everything the hard way and then I will show you the easy way. While good for an emergency it does not beat a good scrubbing and oiling. Everyone grabs a brush and heads for the lake. You do not need anything else, just a brush.

Why is it warm here?

It is a pocket dimension. That's why. Do you want it cold?

No.

With the exception of silver and whites neither do they. There are changing rooms and bathing suits for everyone.

You don't have my size, says a small little russian.

The girl is too small for an adjustable bikini. He waves and a two piece appears.

I prefer a one piece.

Happy!

Thank you. She runs to the water

Don't forget me Sam pops up.

Shorts I take.

Yes

You know I can magic you into one gender.

Mercury tried. He thinks it has something to do

with who my mom is that prevents it.

Who is she?

Laura something. Just showed and left me with

a note.

Did Mercury test you blood?

Yes, and he said all he could tell me was it not

Greek and Roman. Based on my looks he

thinks Celtic or Norse.

I will check later. Cause if it is what I think is happening you may not even be mortal.

Is that a joke? Do you want to hear a story or clean Sparkle? He waves his hand and bikini top and shorts appear. Go clean her and we will talk about why she suns herself.

Ok I am holding to that. I better go.

Do you think she half-breed Calypso asks?

The Eye of Fate thinks so based on the hair I pulled from her clothes.

You should tell her.

Why is she different enough and trying to fit in.

Look at Sophie. If I didn't know better I think they were sisters.

That is not good Calypso says.

Sophie is launched into the air.

It's fine she is laughing. I am worried not the girls. Zach and Sky are snuggling in the sand. Unless you two are planning on getting married then back it up.

Party pooper they say.

They seperate. Buzz Kill.

Get married and then you can snuggle all you want. Remember your both deities so Ma'at got you to do it. Remember what his fate is. To love Love.

But you changed Fate before by giving him the sword.

I did that because we needed help to win a war. Not cuddle on the beach. My point is if you seriously summon Ma'at you can wed. Just know that he will constantly cheat on you once he meets Love.

What does it have to be that way.

It shows fate written before anyone.

Hephaestus is the only one to remember why.

Fine I'll wait

When do I meet this love girl?

When Clotho sets things in motion Athropos wills it in being. Right now she is happily married to Hephaestus. Back to cleaning dragons. Soon everyone is sunning on the beach. Everyone imagined all the dirt, sand, and grime appearing on the beach. Draw on your dragon power and repeat

clean and neat

wash and repeat

That's a lot of dirt.

Yep.

Why? We always do this, Gustof asks.

Because it is lazy, if it doesn't deal with bugs or if your dragon is hurt if you're looking. Your dragon will let you know through excessive scratching or complaints than it time to use it. Grab some oil and start oiling every scale has to be done. Rufus' light touch was not so rough he might bite. Sophie is good with the eye scratches, Silva likes it.

Small good for something.

Oiling continues until lunch is called. Small dragons perch on stools to be fed. Everyone eats roast beef or venison.

Hiro walks over and says I am a fish eater.

See the woman with the horn. That Calypso, tell her.

He walks over and demands fish.

This isn't Japan, please get you what you want.

Please may I have some fish. Fish appear. Domo. He walks off. Any more special requests. Some Asian kids come for rice and fish.

Just so everyone knows after this meal there are no more special requests, Martin exclaims. I will try to make sure enthnic guidelines come into play. Magic has limits to what items it can produce. You have to be able to live off what the local land provides or what you individual magic can conjure. I think that will be tomorrow's lesson, conjuring food. After lunch our Dragon knight went over to weapon and battle sorcery.

Why battle magic?

How many of you here today were offered jobs in your government if you had a dragon. All raise their hand except Sophie, the Gods, his kids, and the sickling. You all technically belong to me. I can stop you from working for your government. I and Erik will banish all you to a pocket dimension before we see another dragon war. Am I understanding?

Yes sir everyone says.

Through the portal is the battle arena.

First Half-pint versus Silva.

The object is visualized, vocalized, and executed.

Offense and defense magic only.

Begin as the gong sounds.

Frost ray SIlva.

Half-pint dodge and fireball.

Try something out of your elements.

Lightning Fury calls Sophie and Lightning encircles Half-pint.

I guess I win.

You did well. Now eat and rest your dragon exhaust.

Poor Silva. How about a side of beef as it conjured out of thin air.

Next Prism and Sparks.

I claim unfairness. He got more aggression than me.

That's how the cookie crumbles.

Dancing Lights. The whole arena lights up in prismatic lights.

Trying to blind, that is a good tactic.

Ring of Fire

Prism dig. The fire goes out. Tackle and kiss and him. He kissed into submission.

Unfair.

You are the one that could not block the attack.

Sparkle and Frost you are up next.

This is definitely unfair, he got an elemental advantage over me.

All the more reason to counter with none elemental moves.

Ice Storm

Energy shield. A shield forms in front of her. She chants and her and her dragon disappear.

Snow Storm; as large flakes of snow gather on the invisible dragon.

Iron Bands

Frozen Skin

You two are definitely evenly matched, we are going call this a draw. They both bow. The matches continue for the rest of the afternoon. They head back to the Grove to eat a wonderful oriental meal served by the staff. You have 2 hour free time. Anyone with letters that need to be sent. I want them by then. A dozen messages go the way of magic birds. Sam comes up with Sky.

Can I install a satellite dish so we can watch tv?

It is not going to work here.

Conjure a crystal ball and watch that or better yet read a book. Sky can you give us a minute.

Sure.

Sam we talked earlier are you ready for a story.

Sure.

Roughly 4000 years ago a God was found on the frozen wasteland. He was raised among the other Gods. He despised them. Eventually he had all manner of children from normal to beast. There are rumors that he is said to be the father of some and mother to others. He even has children of both genders.

You think I am one of these children.

We can ask the Eye see and she was it has to say.

I could pluck a hair and confirm or deny everything.

What will it tell you about me?

Everything about you are and what you could be.

I thought my fate was set the day I got chosen.

One choice is who this child is and their mother is coming and not for the good of the academy.

Now battle training makes sense. I guess to rule out the possibility.

He plucks the hair from her head and touches the Eye of Fate. Her life unfolds again to see her birth by a man. All the way up to the possibility of being queen of Asgard. You are definitely his daughter.

Who?

Loki.Here all that I know about him up to his escape from Asgard.

Thank you.

 I am here for you

What I need is for anyone I can have without revealing my secret.

You want love.

Yes of course. You Mercury are the only one that knows my secret and you are both taken.

Talk to Calypso and see what she thinks.

Ok see you later.

Eye of Fate reveals what is hidden.

You fear a plot.

Always one never knows.

Yes Sky. I see the invisibility is working.

What is her secret?

Ask her.

She wrapped tighter than a top.

Still have to ask her.

You do realize spying is wrong no matter the reason.

Sorry.

You owe her the apology, it was a story you spied on. Even if you're an aspect of Fate you still do not get to know everything why there is a balance to things, Would you like me to tell everyone how your father molested you.

No I would not.

Then either talk to her or respect her privacy.

But I am concerned.

But you're not doing it right.

Concern people ask questions. Nosy people snoop. Being invisible and eavesdropping is definitely snooping.

Yes sir.

Catch her why there is still free time. If she does not find her call me and we will look together.

Yes sir and she takes off.

Chapter 6

Yes Sophie.

Sorry I am late but here my letter. He sticks it in a tube and it is gone. Here your mail, don't rub it in but you're the only who got mail.

Did you read it?

No.

Can you.

Why?

Cause I can't read. I am 8 and still new at it. He reads the letter to her. I am worried sir, could the Russian Government go after my family.

I can only see your fate and it has nothing to do with the government.

That's good.

I keep watch on everyone.

You still have an hour of free time, I can take you home if you want.

You know it late there. Still seeing my parents would be great. He opens a portal. I told you they all sleep.

Wanna wake them.

Just mom, I need to let her know that I am safe and ok.

Lead the way.

She leads him to a small room. Mom.

Oh Sweetheart you should have told me you were home. I would have stayed up.

It Ok

I want to let you know I have a room as big as the whole house.

Your kidding. But I share a washroom with Sky. She is one of the other girls. Oh I have to leave, I only have an hour. Soon I have more.

Show me the ripples, Martin says as he holds the Eye as he watches fate reveal itself. Perfect Fate chosen. Here ma'am here some gold to help your family. Ready Sophie.

Yes Sir. How much did you give them?

Enough to feed them for 10 years and get a house big enough none of the siblings will have to share. Now I see why they were so eager for you to go.

Yep it crowded. As a girl I am worthless to them.

You're not worthless to me. Come here, I have a gift for you. Ready it going to be a head rush. He touches her forehead. Language hits her brain like a sledgehammer. Now you can write or read anything in english or russian.

Thank you. She runs off.

Yes Sky.

I can not find her.

He focuses his energy. She is by the lake . Do you want me to come?

Yes please.

They poof to the lake. Sam, someone needs to talk to you. Do you want privacy?

No! Can you get out so I can at least pretend you're paying attention.

Fine. What up?

I am sorry. I screw-up early. I used magic to spy on you. Because I was worried about you. What are you hiding that got you so stressed?

Why spy from the start?

I am an aspect of Fate, when something is hidden from me I like to find out why. No one wants to talk to me.

Well we all have secrets and you can't know everything.

Someone reminded me of that when he caught me.

What is your secret Sky?

You do not want to talk about yours, so why should you ask about mine.

Fine.

I was molested growing up. But please do not tell anyone.

I won't. She whispers in her ear.

Really, How does that work?

It's too complicated to explain. Ok

You two are better, because it almost lights out.

Yes sir they say. They go walking to the quiet places.

He opens his senses and locates everyone. He also locates a helicopter landing in the outside of the Grove.

Who is in charge here.

I am Martin Seelie

This place lights up from space.

Funny. Can I help you?

I missed you at the choosing.

Who are you?

The President of the United States!

Since your school is in US Terrority I was

hoping for a little quid pro quo.

I can move it, I got four other places picked

out. Do you really want to pick a fight with

God?

I could just Nuke the place.

It will be moved before you could even open

the football.

Where to?

Ain't telling.

Fine, but I need a favor.

What is that? I was away at the choosing and my daughter Mina wants a dragon.

Dragons choose their own partner. I have an angry council of the Gods to prove that.

Please just let her try.

Fine if she gets chosen she can stay here to learn how to care for her dragon. How old is she?

16

She'll fit right in.

Mina came out. Mr. Seelie is going to try and get a dragon.

Just reach in.

It feels empty. Hey a rock just jumped in my hand. She pulls out a white egg. A head pops out.

That is snowflake. Mister President, While it was nice, I have kids to put to bed. Don't bother coming back, we won't be here in the morning.

He kisses his daughter and boards the helicopter. Soon he airborne. Thank you. I am free at last.

I removed and short circuited 4 tracking devices .

4 there are only supposed to be 3.

I removed 4.

Are we really leaving as soon as everyone is in bed?

Yes.

He tucks Caleb in bed with a kiss.

Night Dad.

He tucks Cady in bed with a kiss.

Night Dad.

He tucks Sophie in.

Night Sir.

He checks on Mina.

It is great being out of the White House and no Secret Service.

I am better than the Secret Service, I know the future.

If you know the future then why the choosing.

Dragons are chaos creatures and aren't bound by Fate. They choose who they want.

Oh.

Get some sleep, I have to prepare us to move.

Yes Sir.

He heads to the Grove tree and starts to chant.

Watching the Grove move in tree and space.

He sets a better cloaking spell. Try and find me now. He meets Calypso. Why even let her choose. The new ones are not prepared for a fight and that is how it would have ended.

Let's get some sleep, you seem warm.

Ok.

Chapter 7

We've been going over the same stuff for a week. Cleaning and magic.

What else is there to learn?

Combat lances are the main weapon of a dragon rider. Until you are able to mount a dragon there is little point in learning about any of that. I will show you. This is a dragon rider's lance. It is magical and 30 feet long and weighs next to nothing. I have a factory turning out thousands of theses this time next week. Soon you will be practicing with them. Until sorcery and cleaning is all there is for you. Proper dragon care is essential. Unless of course you want to learn first aid.

Yes they all scream.

Rule one: Always portal somewhere safe before starting any first aid. The Grove is the best place, followed by Avalon or Stonehenge. If you find and cloak a safe landing site it might be a place to go. As a last ditch effort you can create a pocket dimension. Questions? Good I will go over all kinds of injuries and go over both magical, mundane, herbal, and divine. He simulates all kinds of injuries and comes to the solution to summon Mercury for first aid training. Then he shows them how to plant

and maintain the garden. He gives them a garden plot and seeds to grow their own herbs. After a week or two we will see how everyone is doing and what you can trade amongst yourselves. Go plant why I set up lunch. Yes you can work in groups. They cheer. Break up into groups. He sees Zach, Sam, Sky, and Sophie working a plot. Gustof, Lance, Ken, and Rufus pick hard ground to work. Mina, Melanie, Mary, and Mike work by shore. Hiro, Taylor,

Caleb, and Cady pick a spot in the center of a clearing.

He sets out a picnic lunch and waits an hour to call everyone for lunch. You all have the ideal spot for some herbs. There is no ideal spot you can pick for everything to grow. Pick your herbs carefully and ask questions. Go have fun. Why are you planting so many Sunflowers Sky.

Something is telling me to and I can't explain it.

Ok. It will reveal it itself in time. Gustof why so much wheat.

To make beer dah.

Ok you know I have a bottomless cellar.

Really. Yes I still make German beer. It is better.

Ok. Mary why periwinkle. Good for winter wounds.

Good choice.

Hiro, where are you leading me to?

We are setting up the clearing to get good light and minerals from trees.

Good plan. See if you can plant by the willow trees by the clearing. Harvest the bark, I will show you how to powder it. It is a good pain killer for all things. He lets the plants and everything then summons a light rain. Some of the girls dance in the rain and men complain. It's good for you and you can dry it with a thought.

Really how?

Imagine, vocalize, and act. Water is pulled from the men's clothes.

Look they can't handle a little water.

This is not a little.

It barely rained enough to wet the ground.

At least the water is clean and no one is wearing white Gustof says.

No it is dirty work that is why most of us wore jeans.

Lets head back for dinner and see how the garden grows this afternoon.

You're planning something. That's why we're leaving for dinner.

Yes I am Sky. On the table is first aid kits for everyone and a book on what to do first aid wise. Let me know if you want more info. You notice empty slots in your bags for the herbs you grew today. We will harvest after dinner. I hear clean spells going off as dinner is served.

Sir

Yes Sophie.

Can I be the Dragon's Vet.

Of Course. There is a lot of work to it.

I am ready. I wanted to be a vet but this seems

cooler.

Ok I will get you the books.

Thank you.

I think she'll do fine.

How do you know what I was thinking?

I just know you.

She got a kind heart. She'll do good.

I guess I need an infirmary for her to practice

in.

Probability help.

I make one doing free time.

Good

You are on mail duty.

Nothing that I saw but I have not been in the office yet.

I'll check you eat.

I'll be back.

Mina is found trying to open the office door.

Aren't you supposed to be eating.

I did.

You know this is off limits.

But I need to know where we are?

Somewhere on the Earth that is all you need to know.

The landscape changes everyday.

Because we move every night. That stuff that started with your father can not be repeated, For someone to threaten to nuke the Grove is unforgivable. If it was not for communication with people's family we would have moved to a pocket dimension. So don't snoops. I know your father wants the location but it is a secret. Even from me. I am not even sure Martin knows.

Why?

Cause sometimes that just magic how magic works.

Oh.

Have to be not what you want to be.

Oh.

So go get ready for class.

Yes Ma'am.

She hurries off as she mentally communicates with Martin about the situation with Mina.

She gathers the mail and puts it in a magic bag. So she joins them as they head back into the garden.

You accelerated time Mary says.

Just 6 weeks. But everything can be harvested so I will show you how to prep it for your use and Erik will instruct you on use and placement. They go around picking and harvesting. Martin offers pointers to take leaves, flowers, berries, or roots. After everything is harvested they step in a work room with drying racks, mortar, pestle, scales, flasks, and vials all to use.

Your group needs to use the book, trade and bargain to make whatever cures you can. The group with the most cures gets to pick tomorrow's lesson. They rush to complete the assignment. Stuff starts to dry over a low fire.

Hiro how much willow bark did you harvest.

5 pounds maybe a little more.

Trade with Sky for some her Sky Bloom Flower and I will show how to make a potent pain killer for your group.

Cool. He approaches Sky and starts to wheel and deal. Coming back to the group with flowers.

this is how you powder willow bark, then add a petal and freshwater. Mash it into a paste or liquid depending on how you want to use it.

Thank you sir.

He shows Sky's group what to do. Lance looks like you're missing St. Johnsons worth doing any real work. I know but thanks to Gustof all we have to trade is wheat. See those pods.

Yes there are just weird peas.

It is a Moon Pod. Just one of them can get you started. No one else has any. They needed to fix a number of dragon illnesses. They only grow in the cliff area. Trade with everyone to get started. Gustof screwed up. Too much wheat, not enough herbs. I see that now. I helped Lance get herbs but you to prepare. You could have grown enough good herbs to win this competition. Mina you grow a lot of periwinkle but you need to be combined with something hot like fireweed or arrowroot.

Yes sir. What about menthol or mint.

To cold unless your treating frostbite and magic is better for that less chance of losing a limb.

Yes Sir.

How your Sunflower experiment.

Someone seemed to like roasted sunflower seeds.

That's funny. Dragons get there when we are making decisions. What are you making?

Poison.

Why?

To fight dragons bane. You have to make a cure for it.

Just be careful of that. It is dangerous.

So what the ground lotus extract for. You know if it is the cure for what I think it is, Using the whole flower would be better. You know werewolves are not real.

People say Gods aren't real either. But werewolves have nothing to do with it. Right there is what I am curing.

Scale rot. That's new.

Not Really. When they brought the Moon Pod over, I looked up the uses and what I had the most of. Here we are.

Time is up. Just turn off the flames and everything till tomorrow after Dinner. Let's see what everyone makes. Sky.

My group made 5 dragons bane, 3 feverfew, 11 all purpose painkillers, and 6 scale rot cures.

Gustof

Just dragon rot cures

How much?

10

Everything we traded for we know nothing about. Most of us are not good at book stuff.

It's ok you'll get plenty of practice.

Mina your group.

7 muscle rub, 8 frostbite cure, 14 cough remedy.

Good job.

Hiro

25 painkillers in different degrees and types.

Good we have a tie. Sky's group decided on the morning lesson. Hiro you get the afternoon lesson. Let me know by the end of my free time. Pick up your mail from Calypso on your way out. Mail gets passed out. Martin heads to the cave opening and starts working his magic inside the cave to hold a 100 adult dragons at one time. He then makes an alchemist station for mixing medicine and a sterilizer for instruments. He sends a message to Sophie to meet him at the cave.

What is up buttercup?

I am not a horse.

Let me show you, your new work area. Out that back door is a grove for growing herbs. It is ideal for just about every kind of herb but those that require cold to grow.

Thank you sir.

It's your job to grow and stock it all as you learn what to do. Anything you need just ask. Seeds are in the jars in the corner shelf. She sets off and he leaves her to it. He sees everyone lounging under trees reading but Sky, Taylor, and Sam. What up with my 3 outcast Musketeers. Trying to come up with a good lesson. Hiro wants to expand on creating items and cooking for yourself. Not a bad skill to have. Basic ingredients require less energy after a fight that might be important. Why prepare for a fight. I got over a thousand eggs still to hand out. I know there's going to be fighting plus mating flights. The males fight to breed. Fighting is not going to stop just because I will. All I can do is prepare everyone. Then there the renegade scenario.

We get it. What about mounted combat with what.

Swords or guns.

Both.

We can have a marksmanship class.

Cool.

I will set it up in a pocket dimension in the morning.

Good see you there.

He finds Hiro. So cooking.

Yes who spilled.

One of the girls.

So it dum

No it not, it could save someone's life.

When you have little energy left.

He walks in the dining room to pile of mail and starts to send it all. Finds a letter from Sky to her Dad. Using magic he reads it. He may have to pay a visit to him. See if he can cut the ties that bind her to him. He sends it.

So what is up husband of mine.

Just some of these letters.

What about them?

Half talk about working for the government and the other half talk about saving the world. One of the adults is even planning on doing magical hit work.

That is a joke right. No, he sent a letter to the company to see if they were interested.

What are you going to do?

See what the Eye of Fate has to say and go from there.

Maybe we should focus on other groups.

Fate decreed who to focus on. It shows how some of the eggs were chosen.

Ok I get that but you still need to spend time with the other classes and give speeches on why we don't fight.

Ok I'll try.

Good.

Let's head to bed.

They go to leave and Sophie runs in. Am I late?

Let me have it. He touches it and poof it's gone. There you go. I guess you will get a response tomorrow. Because you know it late.

I know.

I will let you know if there is anything after breakfast.

Outside Mina cast on the Grove Tree, Are you trying to be the first one banished to a pocket dimension. Not just trying to alert my father where we are.

Not just trying to alert my father where we are.

You know you're falling.

I already removed the cloak.

I control your magic and you think after a few weeks you can defeat me.

But.

But Nothing. Once you see why you don't want them to find us.

Show me.

Welcome to Void. There is nothing here but us.

I control everything coming and going Mina. He can't find you. Cause you are nowhere.

But.

I hate that word. So be a good girl and learn and prosper. You have a good future if you take it.

What is it?

That I can't reveal Fates about non interference.

Bummer Snowflake loves you, stop thinking about dissecting him.

But how.

He is part of you. If he dies so do you.

That was not part of the deal.

If you made the choice you know that.

But why didn't you say something before.

Because you would not have been chosen and snowflake would not have been born. I need to go somewhere. Anywhere but here.

You can't leave till the 10 months are up and the dragons are old enough.

Accelerate time.

Nothing would happen to us and we still are the same. It only works in the pocket dimension and on plants. Really only the Master of Time can make you older but you still have not learned enough to take care of a full grown dragon. This weekend if you are good. I 'll send you home for a visit. Cool but you got to be good.

Why bad is fun?

You're not cut out to be a brat. Spoiled yes brat never. Ok he lowers them to ground. Satisfied.

No but you can't help that. Free time is over. It is almost time for lights out. They head off.

So how desperate for Daddy's approval .

She hurt everyone even herself. Did you know she wants to dissect her dragon.

What?

I explained to her that she died too.

That's good.

She is still going to try.

Why that?

Because now she is curious.

What are you going to do?

Hurt her dragon and watch as she feels

everything.

That means.

But necessary.

Necessary was your old life.

Can't make them relive the past.

I might try it.

Try it first.

Ok

After class tomorrow.

Lets get some sleep.

Chapter 8

Sam knocks on the do around midnight. Sir something wrong with Sparkle.

I will be right there.

He dresses and walks to the next room. Go get Sky now. She runs from the building. They return. Where is the DragonBane you brewed?

In my pocket.

Check to make sure it's all there.

It is here.

Though the incomplete doses are in the Cauldron.

He opens a hole and the Cauldron is missing.

Can you help? He pulls a Moon Pod from Lance's workstation.

If there is a cure for Dragon Banes why not just tell?

It is not a cure. Just a bandage to keep it from worsing. She has to fight it herself with your help. Let's just let her rest out here. Dosing every 2 hours. Try to stay calm.

Who did this she asks?

I will find out who. I have my suspicions. I'll look into it and let you know. He rings the bell to start to summon the students. Students in the mess.

Someone stole from the lab and did not know what they were doing or why. The only thing I can't figure out is whether it was accidental or not. There are 5 suspects and 5 bottles. The suspects will spend the night in the bottle dimension to see what it's like to be imprisoned which is going to happen if the pair dies. As I call your name step forward. Sky, Gustof,

Mina, Sophie, and Lance. Unless someone wants to confess you will all spend the night in the bottle why I investigate. You either leave the bottle as I clear you or in the morning. Questions? Good. He waves his hand and they disappear. Let this be a lesson to all of you. I take the health and safety of everyone seriously. Back to bed. No class tomorrow.

He heads to the lab to watch the time loop provided by the Eye. He starts to follow the invisible character as he does Sam's meat tray. Following him out to the Grove tree where he dumps the rest and sees himself looking down. He follows him to the male dorms walking into a linen closet. Gustof comes out.

Maybe he will take German beer seriously.

So as I feared. Rotten. He walks back to check on Sam. Who is curled up in pain. I am sorry you hurt. I do not think you were the target.

I was not.

He did not feel he got enough praise for his beer idea.

Please tell me that is a joke.

No but with hair I can not verify anything. But in the morning I will. Lets tuck you into bed. Lay with me.

Sure.

Calypso stands in the doorway. How are they?

Sick, very sick. The guilty in the bottle for safe keeping The other will be let go in the morning.

Don't keep them too long , we both know what a prison feels like.

I know. I just did not see it coming.

You can't see everything.

He tucks Sam into bed with Calypso. He sits in the corner making something. Soft music fills the room. Everyone but Martin drifts happily off to sleep. He examines Sparkle once again and gives her another dose of medication. Putting her in a healing slumber.

In the morning Sam checks on Sparkle. He better be right.

We have to wait till he wakes up. Ok let have breakfast and let out the other people. He calls Sky first. What have we learned?

Timeouts sucks and don't brew poison someone could steal.

Eat. Sophie: What did you learn?

Don't show people to make a deadly poison just to find a cure.

Mina

That we feel what dragons feel regardless of what is used.

Good. Lance.

Don't help steal deadly poison.

Good.

Gustof. This is your chance for redemption.

I did nothing wrong.

We will see about that. He touches the Eye and watches with invisibility what happened that night. So you did not . Why dump poison in the meat and the Grove tree.

I will be Supreme being then.

No Half-pint was never meant to be a supreme anything. I hope you like the bottle. It is your new home. You're not a threat anymore as he poofs him away.

Chapter 9

Anyone wanting an early trip home line up at the door. He sends everyone home. Only Sam, Sky, Taylor, and Zach are left. Sky and Zach you have God's business to attend to. Yes sir and they poof out. Sam and Taylor the lake is yours as is the garden. I am going to London if you want to get away from this place for a few hours. Yes sir. He leaves them in London and heads for Sky's house. Hello sir do you remember me.

You took my daughter from me.

She has been writing for weeks.

I just burn them.

Why not respond to them?

She can find me if she wants to talk.

You're going to write something along the lines of your piece of crap and she deserves better.

If you think about touching her when she comes home, I will be back. There was paper and a pen. I will deliver it for you.

Thank you for getting her out of this dump she deserves better.

Your Welcome.

Here you go on letter.

Have a good day. He goes to find the girls. Who are in a pub flirting for drinks. Do you girls want to eat or drink the night away?

Can we do both?

Since one of you is too young for pints, I have to say no.

But I am having fun.

Sparkle needs your energy to recover. Let go get a good Louisiana gumbo you and meet Calypso.

Really.

Yes.

Ok,

They poof to Baton Rouge where they meet Calypso.

Show me this gumbo that so good, Sam says.

This way. They park in a seaside plaza. Ordering gumbo that is both seafood and chicken and sausage. They eat and Martin pays the bill. What do you girls want to do?

Can we take the dragons to the park they want to stretch.

Sure why not. There at the park Martin says I am being summoned and I will be back.

The girls play fetch with the dragons and Sam conjures a bone for Sparkle to play with. They start to realize that several adults and children have gathered around. Make them fight, a few kids say. Battle time.

Sam you're sitting this one out, Calypso says. It will just be Topaz and Frost I think Calypso says.

Sparkles come sit with me and we can watch.

Martin appears.

What happened, Snowflake turned the Lincoln Bedroom into an igloo.

Fun.

I see there having fun.

Wish I could.

Sparkle needs time to recover.

I know it's not just her fault she sided lined.

Wanna watch them lose.

How?

Swirl Rainbow Breath. Everything goes chaotic.

Sam laughs at the bunch of multicolor dragons and people. Everyone roars and laughs.

Do you two want to go back to the Grove or stay in town while I visit with my kids?

Do we get cash?

Of course.

We'll stay in town.

Remember someone is recovering.

Yes Sir.

He and Calypso poof out.

So now what Taylor asks?

There's a movie down the block if I remember correctly. Taylor and Sam spend the afternoon in each other's company.

So where to now.

Let's grab an early dinner.

Sounds good.

What are we in the mood for Taylor?

BBQ sounds good.

I want brisket then.

Do they do platters because I am in the mood for everything? They both order platters trays and consume them all.

I guess dragons do really make us eat more Sam says. Where to? The movies, the park, or a club.

Let's club it up, Taylor.

Perfect there one called the 2 Deuces down the way. They start to walk and 2 guys approach. Not in the mood fellows.

Haha. This is are street.

Ice Chains spit out from the wall and grab the guys pulling to the wall.

It Looks like this is are street.

See you later. They walk into the club without even a second look at the ids.

Let dance. They dance for a while until Taylor's phone goes off.

I am out front and do not want to be seen. SO STEP ON IT! They meet him outside. I am calling everyone back. Something has happened.

What?

Later! The 4 of them poof out.

He takes attendance and realizes everyone but Sky and Zach are present. I received several messages from multiple governments to turn you over as dangerous weapons. Any want to tell me how a bunch of half trained dragon riders can be dangerous. I am going to look through time and news clips so my mind as well tells me what happened out there.

A girl steps up. The ice cream man was rude so Flicker melted his tire.

Ok anyone else.

We went ice skating in the park during a heat wave in china.

This goes on for an hour. Before he is satisfied. He drafts several letters to different governments saying that he will hand no one over, but he will not allow anymore home visits till people are better trained. I have gold to repay any of the damages. They just need to be submitted and verified by Fate. He would pay and write the account as teenagers just wanting to have fun.

Chapter 10

He heads to the lake to see it frozen and snowballs being thrown. Calypso is leading one side and Taylor the other. He checks on everyone. Those making, those throwing, and those drinking hot chocolate. Everyone is having fun as a snowball hits his shield.

That's not fair.

Why I am not playing. Just checking on everyone and glad to see teamwork as it starts to snow. There gumbo inside when you're done.

Sam states, did you say gumbo.

Yes, I had it prepped when I saw the winter wonderland.

Cool I am starved.

Lets eat. There is a slow trickle of cold people coming in from the lake.

Finally had enough. Most nods and bowls of chicken gumbo are ladled out. The lake is finally empty.

Sophie rats on Ken about freezing the lake.

It was a group effort. It took 15 of us to freeze the whole lake solid,

Good group effort is important. Now eat up there plenty. Then head to the garden to plant new herbs. He sets a weather schedule, Set the fire dragons to thaw the lake. If you work together it should not take much. The lake is a hot tub and everyone is cleaning their dragons.

You ok Sam

Peachy but I don't want to play.

Let's have a look. There are still traces of the Dragon Banes. But she is fine. Swirl bath time.

He bathes Swirl and everyone watches the giggly dragon. Find that spot and you can do it too. They all try to tickle their dragons and a bunch start to giggle and bellow breath weapons.

There you all go, how to make a dragon laugh.

Good lesson.

Light out everyone.

In the morning I have meetings all day and the lake and gardens. No trouble.

Yes sir they echo. He poof outs.

Sophie looks to Sky, wanna snoop.

You know everything is probably magically locked.

Who knows? Let's look.

Let me grab Sam. The head into the guts of the building.

He was not kidding when he told Gustof it was bottomless.

Should we taste it? It can't be worse than vodka Sophie says.

You had vodka.

I am Russian it was in my baby bottle.

We thought you were Italian.

That's what you get for assuming.

Just like most people here think Sam likes girls because of the way she looks. You don't think that.

I think she likes both. I saw her look at Martin that way.

Sheesh, he is like a father to me.

Sure.

Let move on to what to sample.

Anything red is good in my opinion.

Then pick one.

We only want half glasses because we don't want to be tanked by the second glass.

Each takes half a glass. It is fruity like Sam, Sophie chimes in.

Let's move on. That the lunch bell should go.

We might be missed.

Let go then.

They stagger upstairs and sith with the girls and everything is ok.

Calypso walks over, are you alright.

Prefect they slur out.

Are three stoned or drunk.

We can get stoned later.

So you're drunk.

Don't tell Calypso she might tell Martin.

You are absolutely right I am telling Martin.

Buzz kills.

She escorts each of them to their room and spells the door. She sets magical alarms to check on them in 30 minutes. She makes rounds checking on everyone and securing the cellar. She feels everyone at the lake and heads that way.

Where are the other 3 Mina asks?

Sleeping.

Are they in trouble?

Maybe, I don't know, Martin poofs in.

We need to talk.

What happened?

Sky, Sam, and Sophie were drinking wine from the cellar.'

Ok Sophie is a little young but she has been drinking before based on her liver scans.

You're not mad.

Sky is more than legal based on her country's laws. Sam is about the same age. So no, I am not mad. I am just upset they didn't ask first. But technically I told them everything about the Grove was fair game. A bell dings. What is that?

Remind them to check on them.

I will take care of it then I have to go. He stops in at Sam's who is puking in the toilet. Chewing some mint will help.

That is not what I was expecting.

You're old enough to decide for yourself. Drinking is fine, but doing it excessively sucks.

Thanks oh wise one.

Here some mint. Don't chew a lot of it, it will cut your gums. He poofs into Sky's room. Who is sleeping soundly. I guess she can handle her wine. He poofs into Sophie's room. Who has a towel wrapped around her head.

Why does my head feel like someone pounding on it with a mallet?

Wine has a much sweeter taste and you drank way too much.

You don't seem mad.

I am not. You have a dragon. You've been exposed to vodka and only one of three kids your age and you're trying to fit it. What there to be mad at?

Can you stop the pounding?

How will you learn your limit if I just fix it for you?

Meanie.

How much did you have to drink?

The bell went off on the half of the ninth one.

So tenn cause we snuck one back.

That is a good tally. What a lesson here.

Stop at 5 and call it a day.

How you figure that.

That's how much vodka I can drink before I pass out and puke.

Good lesson.

 He touches her forehead.

It is less intense but still there.

I said a good lesson is not perfect.

If I said not to drink.

I say don't make promises you won't keep.

A perfect answer would I will water my wine so

it does not happen again.

Does it help?

Yes it does.

I'll try to remember that.

Here some willow bark if you chew it, it will

help.

Thank you and he poofs back to Calypso. I am

headed to the UN to discuss the treatment of

dragons and how they are not weapons. He

poofs out. Calypso takes to racing with the

group. They race and Heart wins by a length.

Calypso makes laurel wreaths for her.

What is this?

It shows that you won. What about a trophy?

For a dragon race I think the laurel works. Who

wants a lift contest. They each pick up a stack

of weighted plates. Mike and Caleb go for the

gold as Shadow drops the plates. Calypso

crowns Caleb with his own Laurel. Let's do

swimming next. To the end and back. Glimmer

takes off and leads the pack. Hiro takes first

place and she gives him a laurel. One last test.

Hide and seek. Last one found is the winner.

Green and brown have the advantage. Go as

everyone scatters. Ready to hunt Topaz. This

goes on for a half hour. Melanie and Forest win

by hiding in a tree. What next Calypso? Dinner

then free time. I will hand out mail while you eat. Sky I was told this is important.

Ok Thanks.

She reads it and starts to cry.

What up Sam asks?

Dad says I'm better off without him and not to write anymore.

I am sorry.

This sucks.

If it was not for mint I would agree.

I wish the man would leave for most of my life.

Now he is gone and can't stop crying.

There were tears of joy.

Let me punch you in the stomach and see if those are tears of joy.

Sophie comes over to calm down and my head still hurts.

At least you parents love you.

Maybe that may be true why I am here but if I was home they hate me cause I am an extra mouth to feed that they can't afford.

Sorry.

It was ok . I accepted my place and I got a dragon. My brothers don't.

Good girl don't be discouraged. Let's go to the lake and play since we missed this afternoon.

Fun.

What are we going to do?

I am up for a swim.

You should tell her.

No not is not the time for that.

At the time, we were drunk together. M

Maybe later. They swim.

Announcement says that lights out. They leave the lake. Told you no boys. They head through the mess hall to their rooms. Zach stops Sky, there is an issue and was needed. They all poof out. I guess it's just us. See you in the morning.

Chapter 11

In the morning- I have sad news. I met with the UN. They have banned dragons from Earth. That means no more home visits for the foreseeable future. I am sorry. For what a few did everyone is being punished. The Council of Immortals is trying to find us a suitable place beside the void to reside. Questions.

Can families come here or one of the other pocket dimensions.

It is being discussed. But all of you were photographed receiving dragons. I am not sure what the government will do to your families if they are seen with you.

Can the bond be broken?

Yes, but you would both die in the process. Yes Sophie.

Can we make an island somewhere?

Yes, but we can't keep the dragons cloaked forever.

Oh.

Sorry it was a good idea. Sky come up here.

We have a solution. The Fates have woven a plan, but it will take everyone able to ride and fight.

I have had practice weapons and real weapons constructed. Calypso I need 125 demon banishing rods that are adjustable to fight on foot or dragonback.

I will start immediately.

Thank you.

We have 9 months to make you all fighter, medics, or sorcerers. Report to the training room for weapon practice. He talks to Sky. I saw Sam's future and this is playing right into it.

The Asgardians said they would help.

Good cause only Odin can block Hel's power.

What can I do?

You and Zach can travel and get me a recon report, meeting site, portals, or leadership.

We will.

Snag a hair I will keep watch on you. People return. Martin explains the plan to everyone.

Taylor take a rough shot and write out a schedule for everyone. Sophie you are going to be my messenger bunny that I am going to teach special magic.

But I am little.

That is why this works. It gives me a person here to take care of dragons.

Ok Sir.

Sam you are going to lead from the front. Zach is on strategy. Hiro you are in charge of food and supplies. Mina take a group and start planting the herb garden. I will fix a time loop once everything is planted. Recruit anyone from any class that is not doing something to help you with this. Sky you are her second in command. I am taking Sophie to the infirmary. Make something happen while I am gone. He walks with Sophie. What about to happen is not going to be pleasant. You're going to learn alot about everything related to medical and veterinary science, plus dragons, telepathy, and shielding to boot. Sit there and try not to fall as he grabs both sides of her forehead and concentrates. A few moments laters he stops, how do you feel?

Like the Kremlin just crashed on my head.

It will pass. How do you treat a dragon burn?

Human or dragon

Dragon.

Willow bark paste and silvadene mix.

Good.

How is telepathy?

Fine sounds in head.

Plant your garden and I will set the time loop when I come back.

He checks on the others and sees trees coming down. Calypso has set up a makeshift workshop. He sees people traveling back and forth from the garden. Zach has already set up a command tent and walks in. I will let you know this. I will check tomorrow. But the enemy numbers are unknown to anyone but Hel. How many she can conjure is unknown. If she makes an appearance it will be for me, Odin (Stan), and Thor (Casey) to handle. Just concentrate on the demons.

Sky said 9 months why?

Because at that point the enemy numbers become too big for there to be a small force to handle. So Zach, what do you need from me why I am there?

Their portal sites are the most important. We can't go in as one group.

Ok while I am gone setup practice saddles so people get used to flying. I have to check on the gardens. He walks there to find Mina. So how is it going?

95% planted.

What is left?

Moon Pods in the rocks. I got a dozen from the other classes working on it right now.

What is the problem there easiest to plant?

Just scatter them amongst the rocks and watch them grow.

Here I got them moving rocks.

Lets go fix this. Students move the rocks, just scatter them in the cracks and it will grow.

Yes sir.

Everyone out so I can set the time loop. After breakfast, harvest. In the afternoon replant and just leave it. Do this for the rest of the week.

Everything is planted and a time loop is set.

Good I am glad you figured it out.

I am hungry and conjured food doesn't sound good.

The dining room should just be about up.

Good. Knowledge works up such a hunger.

Go eat the others should be in shortly. He calls a stop to work and tells everyone to come eat.

We are having a camp out and leave your dragons out tonight. See you in the morning.

At the lake they set up 2 person tents with the name of 2 people per tent on them. With the exception of Sam and Zach that have separate tents from the group. The awake in the morning with slightly bigger dragons. Dragons just big enough to practice and ride. I have accelerated things for everyday that passes here, a week will pass at night. First chore is to conjure, cook, or otherwise make your own food. You can also barter and enjoy.

Sam looks at Sky. If you handle some kind of meat I got french toast covered.

Sounds good.

Zach pops up. What can I do?

Water skins for every one and make sure that we have enough water for the day.

I got fresh peppers, he declares.

Soon cook fires and conjured granola bars are eaten. Taylor sets up a makeshift kitchen bartering her cooking skills out for other chores to be done.

How is everything Martin asks.

Schedules for 106 people, rotating through various courses, including cooking class and survival as requested.

What about you?

Feeding 20 people is easy.

Do not burn through your power so quickly, it is needed to last all day and in the field you won't be able to just stop for a recharge without someone taking your place.

I did not think about that. You already bargained away, cleaning up, water fetching, and potion making. You need to know how to make your own medicine for your dragon. I have an infirmary but it is not going to help if you can't get the injured to it.

I see your point. Sorry.

Not your fault. The grunt stuff you can bargain for all day, but lessons you need to attend or all the schedules you made are for nothing. He announces for everyone to pick up a schedule from Taylor.

Sky and Sam go to harvest the herbs and the potions labs to help make medical bags for everyone.

Sophie's in the infirmary drying herbs and stocking medical supplies. She makes a list for Martin to get when he goes into the world.

Taylor works in the potion lab making medical kits.

Hiro, Mike, and Mary hold cooking class for everyone.

Caleb, Cady, Ken, and Lance work on making mundane supplies; pots, kitchen sets, first aid kits, and bedrolls.

In the afternoon they gather for most of the cleaning that did not get done yesterday.

Chapter 12

3 things will be discussed this afternoon. The first is flying, the second is aerial combat, and that last is hand-to-hand combat. First is flying. These saddles have been enchanted to simulate a dragon at flight. As you progress we will move on to aerial combat and combat casting while flying. Questions.

One boy chimes in, I am scarced of heights.

You will get over it, your partner will see to it.

Now climb on and don't forget the leg straps I

don't want anyone falling.

The girls help Sophie with spell work to shrink

everything. Mount themselves as soon as they

can all fly. Use your knees to steer. That and

telepathy can tell your dragon what to do. Put

the saddles down students as lances and

shields appear at each station. As they take up

the gear pads appear on each person. Last

person standing gets a free day tomorrow.

Sam and Sophie kinda. They knock a lot of

people out of the sky. Leaving only Sky and

Zach. They drop Sky fairly quickly.

Zach is going to be hard.

He has a lot of knowledge.

I got something he won't expect. Just keep him distracted.

Ok. She makes a couple of passes as she sees a Sophie falling out of the sky to land on Zach forcing him out of the sky. She cuts the strap as she hits him and both go tumbling out of the saddle. Sam I guess you win thanks to someone's sacrifice. Which shows great team work. You will need that. So you both get a free day. They scream and shriek like banshee.

Everyone hides. Go find them. There are 28 in the woods. They count to a 100. Then head into the trees and immediately find 10 of them. They grab Zach hiding in a bush thanks to his red hair. There you go Erik all collected. Good job girls. Head in for dinner. The girls realize they have red wine instead of juice.

Sam whispers to Sophie, and Sky and both nod.

You have your free time but remember there is no free time in battle so as it gets closer it will be eliminated. Any questions?

One of the girls raises her hand.

Yes.

Will we still get mail service?

Yes. But once we get to Asgard there won't be any till the war is over.

Yes Sir.

Where we are going, we will be sleeping on the ground with your dragons. Everyone is sleeping in tents again. Enjoy your night. The girls take the pitcher and head to the lake.

How do you tent mate Sophie?

I don't know if I slept in the infirmary tending plants all night.

Why? I was working late and didn't want to bother anyone. Just bother Sam she got a private tent.

You do.

Yes.

Why?

It is my secret.

You know you can tell me anything.

Not now.

Ok.

But to stop the secrets is not good.

What is your story?

Unwanted child with too many siblings and not enough food. So I came here. Until Martin opened my mind I could not even read or write. That hard.

Your Turn.

I am an orphan and I have both genders. Yes I am a boy and girl. I lived in the hospital with cancer since my Dad died. I was healed by Martin. Came here and that's why my dragon looks like cotton candy. I never thought of that as the girl laughed.

Zach comes over and asks if he can join.

Only if you hold me Sky says.

I thought you two were not supposed to do that Sophie asks.

Who is going to tell?

I guess no one. They cuddle by the fire.

So what are we doing with our free time.?

I don't know if I really have too much to do to take off. I have things to make that you can't just conjure out of the air. There plants, potions, creams, and doses of medicine. Come help in the infirmary.

I can do that.

Can we cuddle?

Sorry you're a good friend, but you are too young to cuddle.

But you're my sister.

You can hold me.

Why?

I just want you to.

Are you feeling lonely?

A little.

Cuddle with Silva.

Sky cuddles me at night.

You need to grow up.

I am 8 and I can't grow up.

Come here. I keep forgetting how young you are. You do just as much as the big ones. I forget you are the only one of 3 kids here. The other ones have their father here.

I am used to it. She kisses her forehead.

Martin walks up and says everyone looks comfy. Did not I already talk to you two.

It freetime.

Just make sure you are in a different tent.

Have fun.

Chapter 13

As he leaves demons start emerging from the woods. Students start to run. Sam starts barking out orders. People are slow to react. Zach draws his sword and charges. Zach waits as Sky calls out and materializes a staff with an eye on it and follows. Sam crafts a sword and puts her back to Sophie's . Sophie summons a bat and starts to lay demons out. They make their way around camp trying to organize a resistance. They group up in 2 and 3 trying to use hand to hand combat and magic to stop the demons. As it seems there is no end to the horde Martin appears and demons disappear.

Not one person used the easiest and most effective defense. Which is your dragon. They can fight a 100 where you fight in 1 and 2s at a time. This was practice if it had been the real thing you would have been overwhelmed by. Because not one of the 106 people here decided that their partner could fight. I hope this lesson is learned but next time it might be the real thing. Clean up, fix camp, and keep your weapons handy. Dismissed.

He set us up.

Of course he did. We are going to war with demons. They are not going to fight fair. We have to learn to not fight fair. You are Lord of War, you must have some tricks.

There are a few but I am going to need tools and a lot of help. Help we got plenty. First we scatter the camp, we all can't all be grouped. Next we need a watch schedule. Someone always needs to be on watch. Then we will make booby traps.

So far so good. You're thinking something.

Just wish we could conjure some gunpowder.

Why can't we. It's like conjuring a gun. We can make pieces but we can't make a finished product, too many moving parts.

Let's make the pieces and get the younger ones to assemble them.

Sam, supposedly your leader what do you think?

One issue I can see.

What is that?

Sleep!

We can do all of this, but we need to rotate it so people are resting.

Send a message to Taylor, Mina, Hiro, and Mike. We need to divide the camp into 4s so some meet with me.

Sam we need a uniform and rank designation.

That is what I was thinking.

What is a good rank?

Knight which will be the 3 of us.

Like the chess piece Knight. Sophie you the medic corp and we'll get you more trainees but you get a cross with Mercury caduceus in it.

We will put a star in it since you're the leader.

Sounds good.

I think we each need stars to.

That way all the leaders have stars.

So it decided.

The 4 approach. Here the game plan. You're each going to pick 24 people from among the 3 classes and make a flight out of them. Everyone gets 8 hours of rest and 16 hours of work detail until we trained, stocked, and the fight is over. Here are your uniforms. Your knights now. Everyone is a pawn until they distinguish themselves in some way. There should be two extra bodies. Those people should be the best at potions and medicine and they go to Sophie. Also you have to pick 2 to 3 people for field medic duty. You have one hour then 2 flights need to be in bed and other 2 working. Go pick your teams. Red for medical, Black for Mike, Blue for Hiro, Purple for Taylor, and white for Mina.

Questions.

Did Martin approve any of this?

No he wants to launch a surprise attack, we will surprise with training and traps. Sounds good.

Who is in charge.

Us 3 battle wise but the flights are yours to setup how you want. Do you have a plan?

A rough one. We can talk about after you get your flights together. So we can get some sleeping and the rest working on a plan.

Sam you're going to like this but you need to pick a tent mate. Because once Martin realizes there is a command structure he is going to go after the leaders and we need to be ready for that. This isn't some plot to get in Sky's tent. You can take Sky if you want to so long as everyone has a partner.

Thank you, but I will take Sophie just not to knock up Sky. Deal.

You mind as well go to bed it going to be a long day tomorrow.

Tell us your plan so we will know what to expect.

Noone but me will know the whole plan. For you tomorrow, the herbs need to be stocked.

I will deal with booby traps.

At night start stocking, salted, dried, and canned food that will travel well.

Raid the pantry if we were not locked here.

Sophie this is important. I need pocket size first aid kits for everyone.

Yes SIr.

Get some sleep. They all head to bed.

Chapter 14

As Black flight comes in here the 2 paramedics I found in the mix. Names and Dragons. Daisy a yellow dragon named Sunflower. Bruce a blue dragon named Bolt. You two know that your boss is 8 and thanks to magic has all the knowledge you two will need to know about fixing dragons. That should be fine. Ok there is her tent with the silver dragon out front making your camp close to that. You start in the morning.

You 4 as she holds out a hat. Black dots get to sleep. Red dots 16 hours work. Blue dot gets an 8 hour work day. Then a rest period.

What about free time.?

We have a lot of stuff to do and in war there is no free time. Eat in shifts. Have a cooking detail so we only have a few cook fires. Understand. They nod. Hiro picks first, then Taylor, Mike, and Mina. Mina and Hiro end up with black dots, Mike red and Taylor blue. Sam commands in the morning.

Mike have your people start dropping trees and show you what to do with them Zach says.

Taylor I want a 3 foot trench around the entire camp. Get the white dragons to leave the lake but freeze the beach. Yes Sir.

I will be around with pointers for everyone, Sam Comments.

Sky says she is going to walk and see if the Fates see any problems with anything.

Sounds good.

Sky ventures out in the night keeping trees from falling on people, and people from being trapped.

Using a dragon he shows them how to make traps in the woods. Harvesting willow barks as they find it. They made a pile in the middle of the camp of supplies as the night went on that was found, made, or conjured. Soon dawn comes up and the flights head to bed. As Sam directs people to the garden for harvesting and replanting.

Chapter 15

Sophie and the 2 medic techs handle the infirmary garden and stock the shelves with plants, paste, and liquids. Organize supplies from the out. Reconfiguring things to fit the new equipment she requested. Like one elephant size MRI installed in a separate cave. I just hope it is big enough.

How did you get this Daisy asked?

Martin and a whole lot of gold. We are better stock than most hospitals.

How much knowledge do you have? Too much for my age. I have all medical knowledge a God can give. If you doubt me you can quiz me.

It is not that we doubt, we have seen a lot happen with magic. It's just you are my daughter's age and I see what she does with 2nd grade knowledge.

SIlva came out here so we can demonstrate my knowledge. She goes over basic dragon anatomy. As the weeks go one we will get a replica dragon and go over everything.

You really do have a lot of knowledge. I know 2 languages have complete medical needs for both humans and dragons. Yes I know a lot but have no practical skill which is where I rely on you 2 to help me.

Can we get a humankin to practice and everyone can learn together? The field medics report in. All 9 of them. But we can't teach until more stuff gets delivered so it's just making kits today. We need a 106 of everything. Basic 12 x 12. Everything is labeled. I still have everything checked by the full medics. Yes ma'am. The 6 six sit in a circle and assemble lines to make kits.

Sophie conjures soup for everyone.

Chapter 16

48 people work on medical cures for dragons to pass on to Sophie.

Hiro is emptying the pantry of everything that can be smoked, salted, or canned for the flights. He conjures smokers and sets 24 assistants to work. He writes a note about dragon saddle bags will need to be made. Along with portal wagons to carry pots, pan, and other extras..

Sam pulls 10 people from the lab and sets a reasonable watch schedule. Around camps conjures signal fires and alarms. She sets an alarm on the lake.

Caleb comes up to her and whispers. If you can make it happen I am all for it as he takes to the air on dragon back. Erik comes up,

Training time. Everyone not on watch or sleeping needs to train.

Yes, Sir

She gathers everyone but the watch.

Most if not all of your dragons are bigger enough for small flights with you on board. So mount up.

Cady raised her hand. Can I go first?

This is free for all. Last one standing wins.

Come Rainbow it time to fly. She appears and they take off. Soon the air is filled with rainbow color. Burning, freezing and electricity as people as they fall out of the sky and it comes down to Sam and Cady. Cady slings prismatic color like water and eventually Sam is forced to land. Well I think I found my Commander of Sorcery. She has a bishop and star on each arm.

Pick the best 5 of each flight and we rearrange things to make you have a flight.

Yes Ma'am.

I am proud of you.

I am his daughter after all.

I guess go pick your troops and get the dragons to the infirmary.

Taylor you're going to bed, Mike your head to the woods when he gets up. Sure there will be training for them to.

Yes ma'am.

Bishops go on people you pick. There you people treat them well.

I will.

She runs off to help people and pick her crew and gives them the bishop insignias. Soon they were swapping watches and eating. Soon people sleep.

Zach set up a watch on Sam's suggestion.

Sophie finishes patching dragons.

Where clocking out.

Watch out for Caleb flying with a select few with blunted crossbows.

Mainly watching the lake as horn blows. That him and there something coming out of the lake.

Zach hits a gong and people start to form up. They're coming from the lake. Hand to hand combat until the dragons are mended. Then we deal with them.

Two blows come, there on the shore, everyone attack,

Cady and the sorcerer's form in the rear and throw spells as swords clash and arrows fly.

Sophie and the dragons fly in breath weapons blazing. The battle is over quickly as Martin appears.

That better, but you focused on one attack. Wait till you see your camp because you did not there could be multiple enemies. Watch your rear as he faded out.

I can not believe that I didn't see that one coming.

You can't plan everything Sky says.

Sam flys over and does a damage assessment. Sam calls Sparkle and they head for camp. She can smell the smoke before she sees the fire. The smokehouse is in rubble, tents are burning, and the camps are completely wiped out. If anyone has any energy left we are going to be conjuring supplies half the night. Sophie tells Caleb I want double the number of people patrolling airborne and on the ground. Double the watch. Reset any traps that tripped. Double the width of the gap.

Sam you're asking too much from people who haven't even eaten. Been training since noon and fought a combat battle with injured dragons. One task is all they need.

I agree that we need to double the watch from those that slept all day. The rest need to focus on getting stuff for themselves and watch for later. Cause he will be back tomorrow.

I know what you think Sam.

In this order; watch, food, and then comfort.

Sounds good.

Sophie relayed the message.

Done.

As people start conjuring food pots and Hiro with the help of his minions set out to cook for everyone.

Sam, Zach, and Sky start picking both ground and flying watch for the next 8 hours. Men and women start conjuring tents and sleeping bags. Teenagers fill canteens and pots.

Sophie and the medics walk around fixing minor wounds. Making notes to see if we can conjure kevlar and pads for people. She stops at Hiro's fire for food and continues their rounds. Mike and Taylor organize a small group to do clean-up. The night moves on as they finally get Mina and Hiro's group to bed.

Chapter 17

Nothing else seems to happen so they begin resetting camp and get a list of tasks for the day. Including a pocket dimensional storehouse compliments of Sky and her Goddess magic. We need a storekeeper to keep inventory of everything we have and everything we use.

And the pantry is locked so it conjured food for now.

Unless we can hunt it or grow it.

Caleb lands next to Sky. I am going to bed and tell Hiro I want these for breakfast and tosses 2 stags to the ground. If possible I like the skulls as trophies please.

Not an issue. How many are out there.

Couple of hundred on the far side of the trees.

Good you are on hunting tomorrow. 10 big ones should feed everyone.

If you say so. See you in the morning.

Who replaced you Cooper.

I got something for you. You know commander Rook the watch is your baby and so is hunting. Make us proud.

He leaves.

Do you really think putting an 8 year old in charge of the watch is good?

An 8 year old runs medical and hangout drinking with 16 year olds.

Ok point.

Who knows he might be the reason we win again. Because without him we would have lost the water source. Tents can be replaced, fresh water can't.

Ok I get it he did good. Let see if we can find a butcher to handle these deer. He keeps supplying deer we won't need the pantry.

I just wish I could make a cornucopia.

Just keep at it and you will succeed. It's all about focus and power.

I will keep you updated.

I think we should call it an early night for Taylor. They might need their strength tomorrow.

Ok sounds good,

I wish we all had telepathy so it would be easier.

It would be abused. With telepathy comes mind reading.

Why was she picked?

Because she won't pry into anything.

Oh Let's eat. They stop at a cook fire with a bunch of dragon riders

He sits in the tent with Sky going over notes. Another solution is chain or ring armor. We need to find someone with enough information that can conjure it.

Sophie thinks it will cut down on minor injuries.

We still need someone with the knowledge to conjure it.

Let's leave a note for Sam to look there more people awake while she is up then us.

Anything else.

Just someone to conjure saddlebags for a dragon.

Some type of carts dragons can carry.

Ok I'll handle the carts tomorrow. I think I have a plan for them. There are still 3 hours till we swap.

Make a tiny one for Hiro to look at.

She plants the imagination in mind and comes to life. The set on the desk as Sam comes in.

You're early.

Got enough sleep.

Where Sophia? Sleeping like a drunk russian girl.

Is she drunk?

I don't think so.

She just over worked.

Oh.

Can't help that battle conditions will be worse.

Live or die there.

Here it is from scratch. No crack skulls, no gut wounds, and no death.

2 encounters and no death it was either planned that way or we are very lucky and you know Fate does not believe in luck.

I get it. Fate does not believe in chance. So what do we do?

Prepare for the fights and try to win as many as we can with the minimunial injury.

Let's leave everything to Sam and we can steal some cuddle time before bed.

Go, I got this as she fingers the models. This is definitely doable. Saddlebags should be easy. Dragons can do the usual digging. She makes her plan for the rest of the day. Sophie sleepy walks in. Coffee.

Only if you conjure some.

Why?

I didn't make it this morning. Zach and Sky were eager to run. Here are the orders to go around today. Then you can see if one of the cook stations has coffee made.

Ok.

She sends everything and even announces Caleb's promotion.

People start assembling at the cook stations.

They find coffee at Hiro's station.

Sam tells him to smoke half the deer and pass

the other half out to the cook stations for stew

or roast. Just try to stretch it with conjured

food.

Yes Ma'am.

Cooking and lab work are good.

But unhappily that 5 of my guys got snatched

for the watch. Some lose more than that. So be

glad. With the watch requirement doing a 12

hour rotation instead of 8. There are 20 per

shift. The later shift wants more but we can't

deplete the forces.

Think we all said and done each flight will be at

14 unless reinforcements show up. It will be a

week before that happens if Martin gives us

any at all but we will see. When the battle happens the watch will be just as involved if not more than everyone else. Just be glad you're not on trench duty like Mina. He wants it doubled today and I am using every brown and green dragon to it.

Cool.

She went to Mina's camp. So ready to dig.

I am not really a girly girl. I don't do dirt.

You just have to direct the dragons. Today is the deadline, palisades are going up as soon as Zach is up.

I will have it done.

You did pick a lot of brown and green dragons.

I know I was thinking camo, not work.

No place to hide where we are going.

That is a joke.

No it is all rubble.

Not good.

I have to find Mary, do you know who picked her.

Mike I think. If not Taylor.

Sam finds Mike and his people.

Construction really.

I know you want to fight but we need this stuff.

Ok But what for?

Transport food, medical, and other stuff we do not want to waste the time or energy to conjure during a World War. Cause this is what it is. We are to establish a base and work our way out. Then rebuild. So you want to conjure and vaporize blanket and everyday wasting precious energy.

I guess not exactly. Doesn't help that we keep getting smaller. Sorcerer and Watch, I down 10 people.

You can use the sorcerers for construction and it will still improve their magic.

Ok thanks.

I am going to change the flights so that everyone has at least 10 people but I did put out a request for another 100 if not more.

But they're untrained, not sure how that's going to work. I need Mary by the way.

Why?

I have a job for the Queen Dragon she protects.

Ok.

She stars Michael with a thought. That way the kids know you command and won't hassle you.

Chapter 18

Thanks as horn sounds by the lake and Sam is airborne before Mike can blink. Racing for the beach to see a self propelled boat heading towards the beach, Gang planked is lowered and man steps off.

You Sam.

Yes Sir.

This is for you.

She quickly reads it. Here is 250 people ranging from 14 to 24 are the only reinforcements you're getting to use them wisely.

You have a week of no attacks to prepare them. Sophie I need you. She poofs in. Ps you pantry privilege is reinstated for now. Start by telling Hiro to raid the pantry it is open. Wake Cady, Caleb, Zach, and Sky. Get Mike and Mina. All the dragons are big enough but you have to teach them what to do. First question is does everyone know why you are here?

To win a war, they say.

Good.

I know you know nothing. We are going to sort you into categories then break you into flights. The categories are manual work, artisan craft, cooking, military, and those with true sorcery ability. Yes, we have ways of testing you even though you know nothing. Just line up on the beach and have your dragons out. Leadership appears. I am commander of this outfit. I wear a 3 star knight, flight commander wear a 1 star knight. Sorcery commander wears a 2 star bishop and the watch commander wears 2 rook. You will all wear pawns until instructed otherwise. Split is to groups of 25 and we will get the testng over as quickly as possible before lunch. Leaders whisper to themselves and come up with a plan. They spend the morning testing everyone. They end up with 6 flights of 24. 80 people in the watch and sorcery and 21 medical personnel. They summon Lance and Mary as the new flight leaders. Set a sleep rotation where 2 flights sleep at a time. Sam makes executive decisions that leadership will sleep on the same schedule and 2 will be up at a time. They prep the things as the day goes on. Teach new people magic, riding, and hand to hand combat. This goes on for 7 days trying to prep everything, Noon of the 8th day enemies explode surrounding the camp on all sides. Horns blare. If it was for the palisaded they would have been overrun. The watch keeps them to the tree line. Cady and her sorcery corp, flame, freeze, and electrocute things to buy the flight time to take off. Mina sends the greens into the forest and browns to do damage control. Mike takes the blue, black, and white to the lake to make an escape route. Hiro is the savior of the day as his force routes the enemy. Where there is nothing but ash piles. Taylor, Mary, and Lance sweep for the clean-up duty.

Haha. See if you get dinner tonight.

As Martin voices booms over the field. Good job everyone.

The war begins in a week. I will meet your leadership at the

command tent. With all the detail.

Chapter 19

Everyone meets at the command tent to meet Martin, Calypso, and Erik. Here the lay out. We portal to the bridge and clear. We will shut down the bridge by any means necessary. We will use a grid formation to clear the continent. We will then look at other land masses after that and what they need. The Asgardians will be on hand for ground support but remember there only 5 of them. One of them has to focus to keep the portals closed. So we are not overwhelmed. I leave you to do your prep work for a week. Zach I need you to take the red dragons here to help Maylani the new Poseidon.

Yes sir as he steps out of the tent.

Sam says we have uniforms for you 3 too. There here, the King, Queen, and Knight Commander. Thank you. There are demon killing weapons, both hand to hand and lance style for dragon back. Get to work.

Yes sir. Sophie tells everyone to meet on the beach. Their staff and sword size, and even daggers. Bonus is the lance style for dragon back. She gets several clerks to count everything. Get Mike and his flight to start making holders for everything. Taylor and Mina get the wagons setup on the beach. The watch to kill all the wild life they can. Mary and support to make and organize backpacks and first aid kits for everyone. Lance to lab work and last minute prep. Hiro and his flight pantry raid and prepping wildlife for transport.

Soon hundreds of wagons are on the beach. Food is placed in an enchanted cold compartment the Cady fashioned up. Medicine is put in a storage container. First aid kits are laid out for everyone. Regular and silver weapons are packs in the last wagon.

We have a week to be ready and prep work is going as planned Sam states. Thoses that need more practice meet in the clearing. Medical training in the infirmary. Sorcerer training is in camp with Cady. Any questions.

Do you know how long this is going to take?

A month or more. The numbers rage in the millions. But we have 9 Gods to help also.

Are the weapons magical against demons?

Tomorrow I will go over the 3 types of demons we will run into over there but the Queen of the demons is up to the Gods to handle. Yes, weapons are magical against demons. Dismissed to your training to your training. They finish eating and divide into small groups leaving the main camp. The watch comes in and out to eat, flying off again.

Sam summons all the commanders to the command tent. They all trickle in. Zach on some secret mission with the fire breather, so we need an entry plan, perimeter plan, and going through the portal first.

I think that Mike should be followed by the sorcerers. Move Taylor to the left and go to the left. Mina to the right. Lance right and Mary left. Hiro rides the center with the support and supplies. Then trickle the watch in little by little and circle the unit. Medicals can pull the carts through as we clear space.

Sounds good but I want to hold Hiro in reserve to fill gaps and help pull carts if needed. Anyone else has anything.

Just one we still need people on the ground even if the dragons still fly Taylor says.

Why?

Cause there are going to be demons on the ground or even underground. I think we need Hiro and the Watch on the ground.

That is plausible. We got more than enough hand to hand combat weapons. Get Hiro and the Watch trained to use them and we figure out the rest from there and I will join you. Sky, work on food stores and supplies. I want to have everything packed tonight. Zach should be back by then. If there anything we can't make let me know before bed. I'll try to get it tomorrow. Everyone you got your jobs get to it. One last thing promote pawn leaders. 1 sergeant and 4 corporals each. So if needed we can break things down and still have organization. Yes ma'am. Go.

She started to write in her note book that is connected to Martin's stuff. They need things that they can't conjure. She does not want to portal somewhere and get someone in trouble.

That is responsible but no one knows you have a dragon. Just be careful. There is a credit card on my desk for you. Do not take anyone with you.

Yes Sir. She closes the book and heads to the office. She finds a pink mastercard in the center of the desk. She pockets the card and creates a portal. Walking through to Walmart. She starts in the camping supplies. She buys gas lamps, electric lights and canvas tarps. She heads buying soup and snack cakes. She buys everything hiking boots in the store. Head up to the cashier with 2 flat beds and a cart. She checks out and pushes the carts through a portal. She follows through in the middle of camp. Sophie, tell everyone to find a pair of boots that fit. I don't care if they don't like the color. People line up. Hiro your first cause I want all the soup and snacks packed.

Yes ma'am size 12 preferably black.

This is what I got.

At least my holey shoe can be replaced.

I have a long night fetching stuff.

We need a compass.

It wont work where we are going. No magnetic north.

Ok

It takes 3 hours, and they still have a 150 without boots. I am back before dinner and she portals to another walmart. She shops with a list of sizes. She gets more soups and snacks. Heads to the camping supplies and grabs more lights, a camp lighter, and duraflame logs. Heading to checkout with 3 flatbeds. She heads back to camp and everyone has boots and gets Hiro and company to store all the supplies and food. Hiro how the deer? All butchered.

I'll let Martins know that we are ready then. So everyone gets some sleep we leave in the morning. She heads to her tent and pulls out her notebook and writes everything should be ready in the morning.

Make sure you all eat well.

Will do sir. Night

Chapter 20

In the morning Sam has Sophie summon everyone. Hiro and his flight serve food while everyone. Martin walks in the middle of the camp. You all have been training for this battle and it is just a portal away. Once breakfast is over I will open the portal to the small staging that we have set up and defended enough to get you through the portal. Medical staff is staging here. You will have to portal here for major medical treatment. First aid is your responsibility. Weapons are on the beach. Sam will give you your assignments. I guess I will see you on the beach.

Sorry Soph you're staying here.

How do I play messenger then?

I guess I have to do it myself. Cause I have telepathy to.

You are.

Yep. So I will do my own messaging. But I do look forward to throwing you a birthday party when this is over.

You know.

I would not be a good friend if I didn't know that you just turn 9 today. Get your medical people together and have the infirmary ready.

Yes Ma'am.

She kisses her forehead. I will be back when I can. Caleb sends half the watch in the air and the other half on the ground. Mike you are first through setting up a center wedge. The rest of fill in and alternate positions. Sorcerers follow with the beginning of the carts. Taylor second through head to the left. Followed by Mina taking up the right. Mary and Hiro are taking the carts through. Ground crew circles the carts and pushes everything back. Yes Ma'am echoes in everyone's mind. The portal opens and Mike barrels roll through. So everyone

forms on the other side of the portal. Sam says to

start unloading the carts, and camp pitched. Next I

want a trench dug and forest scaled back.

Martin walks up with a tall muscled man. Sam

meets Odin or Stan. You 2 will work together to

bring an end to the plague.

Yes Sir. Welcome Stan. Sam walks off.

So is she the one.

According to Fate.

She is not used to trusting people.

So I have to break through that armor.

Kelvar as a gift should go a long way. Go check

and see what you can do.

He runs after her. Sam brought you a gift to

commemorate our friendship.

What is it if you dare bring me flowers I am going to

gut you like a fish and watch your mantle bleed out.

No, I have kevlar.

Now you're talking my language. How much? 450 vest, 150 odd pieces to protect other things.

Show me.

He takes her where crates are stacked. She sent messages for everyone to come get one. She kisses Odin. This is the nicest gift next to my dragon I have ever got. They trickle in and try on a few and eventually everyone is fitted for one. I got into a battle to organize one. Caleb and the watch report. Wanna help?

Always.

She finds the command structure with the help of Stan. Caleb is already there.

Ma'am they head to the center room. Where there maps already laid out. So what the sky looks like.

We are stuck on an island. There is a bridge that needs to be rebuilt. To use the wagon and ground force.

Give me a guess.

A week to fix the bridge.

Ok what waiting on the other side.

10,000 maybe more. Most of them are ground bound. Maybe 100 flyers.

I don't like those odds. Any chance you could pick some of the forces off.

Maybe. It would be better if Zach was here.

He will be back tonight from the message that I received. He should have an advantage but it will be better with the fire breather.

Ok draw me a plan. You know I am 8 and I don't plan, I'm just going to do it. See what you can do without Zach and we work from there once he comes back. Ok thanks, watch out for the game.

None so far.

Ok keep me updated.

Chapter 21

Caleb and the watch take to the sky. Scouting the bridge and beyond. They pull lances and the 12 riders descend trying to fight what they can to clear the end of the bridge. He Calls to Martin that the bridge cap is secure. You can begin reconstructing the bridge and send me the rest of the watch. More dragons soar in the sky. 68 total of varying color and design. Good jobs get shouted at as they land. Start clearing trees. I want a watch in an hour. Yes Sir. Axes materialize and trees start falling. The strip branches off the trees quickly. Soon the watchtower is set up with a signal fire. 4 men to each tower. Dragons and riders start clearing a path around the bridge. Building a base camp as they drop trees. By the time the bridge is complete.

The watch has a functional camp. Took you long

enough, he says to Sam. One base camp with

palisades to protect the bridge.

Where do you learn all of this?

Martin sent me the information.

Good job squirt. Walk me through the center

building.

That the mess hall.

Why not the Command Center?

Strategically unsound and harder to protect from an

aerial assault.

They listen to you.

They respect me cause I get my job done and

execute it well.

What else can you plan?

Get Zach and I will explain what from the scouts.

They head to a small command building.

You outdone yourself.

You know alchemy, Full blown alchemist that to my dad. Transmutation is my speciality. This is a map based on the aerial recon of the area. This mass is what use to be the palace, temple and royal garden. The portal is the gardens, Neither Hel or Loki have yet to be spotted. I have a 3 pronged attack planned. The flights will do clean up city 4 grids at a time. Part 2 Sorcery squad airdrops into the garden and secures the portal. Part 3 Watch and the Asgardians storm the palace and look for Hel. Zach anything to add. 2 things. First the goal is to get Sam or Stan on the throne. Focus on that and the bad guys will come to us. Lastly has anyone tried to feed a demon to a dragon.

No.

Let the watch know to try it at some point. Might make things a little easier. Sam?

My only question is what is the timeline for this.

I do not plan, I just do. It takes what it takes. I do not know the inside of the palace and therefore can't even guess what the timeline is.

How about an estimate?

3 days maybe a week except for clean up cause there is no estimating that.

You and Zach plan, I am going to find Martin.

Why, I thought you and Stan were in charge of this.

Do you know how to close a portal?

No but sis might.

Can you call her please.

Of course, Cady comes to the command building.

Yes Bro.

What do you know about portal magic?

Too much and not enough at the sametime.

There is a portal in the gardens I need you to seal for me.

What is my reason?

Airdrop.

Oh I did not think so.

It is the only way. Everything around is destroyed unless you think Rainbow can get you around the rubble.

Rainbow says we can do something.

Now it is time for Martin to get approval. Sam called him.

Martin poofs in. What do we have a plan for? Caleb explains to him his plan.

Not a bad son. In the morning we attack.

Sounds good.

Keep the watch on schedule. Everyone else I want to sleep.

Chapter 22

Morning the horns blow. Ground army assembles as swords are drawn. Enemy engagement at the border of the camp. Caleb comes in lightning blazing. Eat your fill boy and let see what happens. Caleb runs the dragon belly to the ground as he swallows demons by the mouthful.

Zach and several others attack with swords. Banishing the demons the one by one until the camp is covered in demon dust. You did well. Caleb will brief you in groups on the plan of attack. Get with the leadership we have until noon. Then we commence the battle. Caleb and leadership will explain the plan. So everyone knows their part. Leadership assembles in the command building. Commands get echoed as sergeants get told to take their flights and clean. Ok Caleb says as everyone assembles. Here is my plan. Flight blue and black will do 5 miles a day clearing the right side. Flight red and purple is left for you. Hiro you on support duty here at camp.

What?

Your flight can operate well out of you. Someone got to keep the supply line running.

What about the watch?

I am leaving 10 here for guard duty. The rest are coming with me. Sorcery will also leave 10 behind . Cady that on you to pick.

Gotcha. Sorcery is headed to the high garden to contain the portal there that we know about. Anyone finds another get a hold of Cady and we will move accordingly. Questions or comments?

Mike raises his hand. Why not split the sorcerer up and look for other portals.

I am not sure how much power it is going to take to close a portal but I would rather have too much then not enough.

Oh

Anything that needs an address before Martin takes the floor.

What does the enemy count Taylor ask?

Too many to possibly count as lights appear on the map. That is what current scouting says for surrounding areas. We were 10 miles out. So there we are. Martin walks up.

This will not be quick or easy, but you have your assignments. If we succeed we have a new home where dragons can roam free. So do your best out there the world is counting on you. You have your assignments, you are dismissed. Taylor mumbles as she walks out.

Problem with my plan Caleb asks.

No, I just do not like being on clean-up duty. It got to be done. But it feels like I am playing second string when I should be playing first.

Look at it this way. If we fail it all falls to you and your group to get the job done. You are the front line. The group has to be small . I am not even taking the full watch. I am taking the leadership, 50 watch members, and the Asgardians.

Parachuting into a courtyard and storming the palace. Can I please come.

Why?

I want to feel productive. Who leads your forces. I have a sergeant.

I'll let you know before we leave. He exits the building.

Cooper, Carter.

Yes sir.

Select 10 men to stay here and the rest are coming with us.

Where to sir. He explains his plan as they listen.

Yes sir. We will have everyone ready in 10 minutes

20 is fine.

Sorcery building Cady tells everyone her plan of action. We are on portal control. 10 of you will stay here. You can all draw lots to figure it out. Here the area around the gardens. Their job is to shut the portal and take over the area. Standard rules say 13 people can clear a portal but this Goddess made this portal so I am not sure. Everyone has been studying the portal books. Any questions?

A hand goes up. What the command structure is why you're gone.

One of the corporeals will be here if you have any questions.

What are the chances of succeeding?

90% barring some unforeseen happening. Why?

Because I want to live.

The medical center is up and running. Everything should be fine. Demon can't stop are weapons plus we have magic as a backup.

In the Command Center. What are you thinking?

That they made this seem way too easy. If his plans work I am hoping it will be this easy. But can it really be that easy.

Stan stopped worrying. He got a good plan and we can succeed with this plan if we just try. How can you be so positive? If part of my nature. Too much has already happened.

It's time for some good. Fine but I want it on record that I think there are going to be problems.

We all think that but it doesn't help to doubt the only plan we have unless of course you have a better plan.

You know I don't.

But I think time is not on our side. So it is better to act swiftly with a plan that might work. Then to not do anything at all and lose without a fight. Stan it alright to be afraid she is a Goddess.

It is not that. She has a lot of my people imprisoned according to the mantle. I just want everyone to come back safely.

That we both do. But we have a plan if anyone gets hurt. Sophie on standby to receive any injury. Let choose are dragons and get airborne. Knowing Caleb he is half to the palace by now.

Fine but I am riding with you.

That up to Swirl.

He laughs.

They walk out to Heimdall sheath his sword. Frigg

and Freya filling quivers with arrows. Where the girl

pretends to be Thor.

Casey with that young dark haired boy with the blue

dragon discussing how to use lightning in doors.

Oh god. She thought with that hammer she was

invincible. So we might be depending on how she

fights with it.

She did do good against the Snake God.

We will see but I still think she should stay with us.

She is young and impulsive. We were all there

once.

She is 19.

Something like that

Exactly.

Let's go find some dragons to ride. Sky what is up.

Sorcery ready and Caleb wants to be airborne in

ten minute. We are on our way. Dragons fill the courtyard.

Carter you have the watch. Yes sir.

At the high garden. The dragons climb through the rubble. Toward the portal, not meeting the creature. Till they reach the gate. Run into a wicked demon 12 feet tall and big as a team of oxen. Sorcery's first squad moved left and attempted to get behind him. As the first squads move left as the monster attacks the center. As they draw batons and scatter. Cady uses Rainbow. She got the best chance against that thing. Rainbow came to play. Sick him girl. Rainbow charges the monster. As they grapple he drops he drops his club to the ground. Rainbow snips as his throat. Monster moves quickly allowing him to be pushed in the garden. The group files. Charlie scans the portal while I try to get that creature into it. Roger that. 3 circles 13 caster each and leave room for me in the center. She poofs on Rainbow saddle. Summoning her lance. They push the creature into the portal. As she dismounts, taking her place in the circle as the group starts to chant in latin. The group outside the circle starts chanting to. So the room fills with a soft chant.

As they enter into the Central Palace. The dragons buzz by the balcony as riders jump from their dragons. Casting slow fall to minimize impact. The first of the watch lands securing the balcony as the groups slowly drop in. All the groups slowly drop in. Should we recall them, Caleb. Maybe we don't want them taken down where we can't help them. Pass it on Copper. Grumble Grumble.
What is that?

Just saying I should have brought Carter.

Oh.

No he is a better spotter, then a fighter.

That is true.

Soon all the dragons are back to tattoo form.

Amber takes points. Someone quietly opens the door.

Even if they know we are here I still want you to be quiet. 2 guys open the door and Amber peaks her head out. Looking both ways. Remembering the map she steps to the left hugging the wall as she waves her people into the hall. Poking a rovering demon with her baton watching it dissolve. She holds a fist up. Everyone stops. She sees three demons guarding a door. Davis, Connor, Alyssa javelins out. As the step in the hallway and throw. Aim is true striking the demon dead center. They continue down the hall. She calls a halt. Summons the Asgardians. This is your show. One or both is on the other side of the door. Roger blows the door. Frank grenades smoke only. 3 second I want the whole room covered.

The portal begins to close as flying demons take off towards the palace. Closing the portal cuts one in half. Caleb flying demons headed your way. About 3 dozen maybe a little more but the portal is secure. 3 down. Copy.

In the medical cave people are teleporting in with all kinds of gashes and cuts. 3 from magic over use. Sophie directs her team like a fine machine. People are triaged and cared for as quickly as possible. Soon she starts to release people with instructions to rest.

Boom the door flies inward as the room is quickly covered. As they file around the outside of the room with weapons drawn. Martin and Odin step in.

Hel you are beaten, leave now back to Helheim

Never Asgard belongs to me.

Thor, Freya, and Frigg weapons drawn. You're beaten as the flying demons crash through the ceiling.

Caleb shouts orders for lances and arrows. Cooper tries to organize people into squads.

Odin and Martin walk towards the throne. Face us.

She walks down the throne drawing a scythe from the air. You can't beat me.

Together we can beat you. Martin draws a sword and Odin a spear. They meet in the center of the floor. The fight ensues as yellow dust falls all around them.

She realizes her demons are dying and she attacks. Martin liquidifies her Mantle as the black mist pulls in the one student named Stephanie. He hands Stephanie a charm and says this will help. You're the new Hel.

Hopefully you will be less evil.

I will try.

Sam it's time to take your throne. Sam walks up the stairs As you sit on the throne. A golden crown appears. She places it back on her head.

Asgard shouts all hail the Queen of Asgard.

Come down here Sam. Frigg has agreed to pass on her Mantle to you. So you can be a true Queen. Just grab her hand. He chants and the Mantle flows into Sam in a green glow.

EPILOGUE

Martin goes to the altar of the Eternal Flame.

Phoenix it time to return to your home to reborn this

world to its previous glory. As the eternal flame

relights as a Phoenix feather falls to the altar.

Relighting the Flame. With Martin keeping the

Phoenix in his hand. Interesting. As the grass starts

to regrow. The world of Asgard is reborn in an

instant.

www.ingramcontent.com/pod-product-compliance
Lightning Source LLC
Chambersburg PA
CBHW021038130626
46552CB00005B/1902